The Susie K Diaries

Show Stopper

Shamini Flint

illustrated by
Sally Heinrich

ALLEN&UNWIN
SYDNEY·MELBOURNE·AUCKLAND·LONDON

For Frans, who stops the show every Friday! SF
For Zara, a show stopper in the very best way! X SH

First published by Allen & Unwin in 2019

Allen & Unwin
83 Alexander Street
Crows Nest NSW 2065
Australia
Phone: (61 2) 8425 0100
Email: info@allenandunwin.com
Web: www.allenandunwin.com

A catalogue record for this book is available from the National Library of Australia

ISBN 978 1 76052 370 1

For teaching resources, explore
www.allenandunwin.com/resources/for-teachers

Cover design by Sandra Nobes
Text design by Sally Heinrich
Set in Gel Pen Upright Light by Sandra Nobes
This book was printed in November 2018 by McPherson's Printing Group, Australia

10 9 8 7 6 5 4 3 2 1

Name:
THE SUSIE K DIARIES'
SHOW STOPPER!

File No. #3

CONFIDENTIAL

Case Opened

This must be Mum's latest attempt to make me the
LAUGHING-STOCK OF THE SCHOOL...

This must be Mum's latest attempt to make me the
LAUGHING-STOCK OF THE TOWN...

This must be Mum's latest attempt to make me the LAUGHING-STOCK OF THE ENTIRE WORLD!!!!

2

What has Mum done, I hear you ask?

4

A SHOW!!!! A TALENT SHOW!!!! TO SHOW TALENTS!!!!!

I HAVE NO TALENTS TO SHOW!!!! ZERO! NADA!!

Unless...just maybe...knowing lots of words that mean 'zero' is a talent?

My mother is the best mother in the world...

She loves me...

She encourages me...

She believes in me...

There is only one PROBLEM. She has no idea who I am...

7

Mum thinks I am as POPULAR as Beyoncé!

Me

Beyoncé

She thinks I am as ATHLETIC
as Serena Williams!!

Me

Serena
Williams

She thinks I'm as musical as Beethoven!!!

And now she wants me to be as TALENTED as...

My name is Susie K. I am nine years old.
I don't want to be in a talent show.
I have no talents. Even if I had talents, which
I don't, I don't want to stand on a stage and show
them off.

I just want to be left alone with...

Bones, my model skeleton.

He doesn't talk much and I like it that way...

Or George, the school goldfish.

(There aren't many pets out there for someone as allergic to fur as me, so now I've basically adopted George and he comes home with me most days.)

And my crossword puzzles...
At least my hobbies help me forget my troubles!

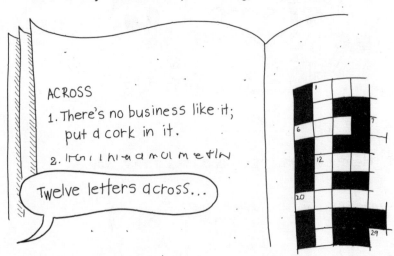

It looks like I'm going to have to be HONEST with Mum and tell her I don't want to take part in a talent contest.

Just kidding...

I could never tell Mum something like that.

How sharper than a serpent's tooth it is
To have a thankless child!

You see, Mum was a child refugee from Sri Lanka, and she wants me to have all the opportunities she never had as a kid.

This makes it very difficult to have normal conversations with her.

It doesn't matter what I say, she always has a horrible story to tell me.

16

AND Mum wants me to be a HUGE success at everything I do. She wanted me to be popular and sporty and now she wants me to be a HUGE TALENT... IN A TALENT SHOW!!!

And I don't want to disappoint her because she's my mum and I want her to be happy...

Are you going to do Shakespedre, darling? I think he's the best playwright who ever lived.

When I was young, I loved Shakespedre!

Unfortunately...

NOOOOOO!!!!!

Let me guess, a bomb fell on the: 1) theatre 2) library 3) bookshop?

I will admit that I did not see that coming.

That's more like it.

Years from now, instead of the emperor's new clothes...

Or the ugly duckling...

Or the princess and the frog...

People are going to be telling their children and their grandchildren about THE GIRL WHO WAS THE LAUGHING-STOCK OF THE WORLD.

Unless I find a way to solve this problem...

And that, my friends, is exactly what I am going to do!

BECAUSE I am a PROBLEM SOLVER!!!!

Even better, I already have a system that works.

The method to solve all problems, whatever they might be, is exactly the same...

1. IDENTIFY THE PROBLEM

That's easy...Mum wants me to be a SHOW STOPPER!!!!

2. ANALYSE THE PROBLEM

I don't want to be a SHOW STOPPER. That wasn't so hard either.

3. FIND A SOLUTION

Mum might think that a SHOW STOPPER is someone who performs incredibly well, but what if I ACTUALLY stop the show?

How do I stop a show?

I know...

I will lock the doors to the hall and throw away the key...

I know…

I will set fire to the building after school in the middle of the night…

But what if the fire spreads from the hall to the science labs or the library!!!

That's a risk I can't afford to take…

I know! I will just pretend that I forgot to sign up on time...

I'm sorry, Mum, I so wanted to do the talent show but I forgot to sign up in time.

I'm so0000 disappointed!

I signed up for you, Susie K.

I know how forgetful you can be!

You don't have to thank me...

I'm just so proud...

29

The next day at school...

31

32

And I'll be the most surprised if I can think of something to do.

Maybe I should run away from home so I don't have to do the show?

Just George and Bones and me...

But what if they find me just BEFORE the SHOW??

Maybe I should stay hidden in plain sight... and no one will find me before the show??

Maybe I'll pretend to be sick??

36

It looks like I'm going to have to do the talent show. Which means I need to DISCOVER a TALENT.

There's no need to panic, George.

Panic is a smoke raised with the fume of sighs...

How hard can it be to discover a talent?

After all, no one's asking me to discover gravity like Newton did...

No one's asking me to discover penicillin like Fleming did...

No one's asking me to discover the South Pole
like Amundsen did...

All I have to do is find a
teeny-weeny, itsy-bitsy talent!!

A little research
and I'll find a
talent in no time...

The next day...

It's time to have a look
at what the other kids
are doing. Maybe I'll
get some ideas for
a talent, George...

Still...how hard can it be to sing?
Maybe singing is the solution.

4. TEST THE SOLUTION.

43

45

Maybe singing is not for me, George.

Back to the drawing board.

It's time for more research.

Let's see what the others are doing...

5. REPEAT UNTIL THE PROBLEM IS SOLVED

50

51

Back to the drawing board...

singing
dancing

Will you be playing a musical instrument, Susie K?

You're like a one-man band!

You've had lessons in so many!

I remember those lessons well...

There was that time I was learning the violin...

NO TESTING ON ANIMALS

STOP ANIMAL CRUELTY!!!

CATS HAVE RIGHTS TOO!!!

MY DOG WILL BITE YOU...

AND YOU DESERVE IT!!!!

Grrr!

Mum had to explain...

Or that time I learnt to play the drums...

Mum had to explain...

Or that time I learnt to play the flute...

and for some reason all the small children in the neighbourhood followed me home.

61

Today I'm going to do my research in books.
The real world isn't safe.

63

He's right, though.

I really have NO TALENT.

More research...

A good problem solver doesn't abandon the problem just because the first few solutions were duds.

Mind you, I'm running out of time and everyone else seems to be doing well...

Except James.

75

What are you going to do?

A maths puzzle on stage?

Or a science experiment?

Or read a book?

Maybe I will, so there!

THE EUREKA MOMENT

85

SHOWTIME!!!

Mum and Dad are in the front row.
Why am I not surprised?

I peeped through
the curtains.

The other kids were
doing very well.

88

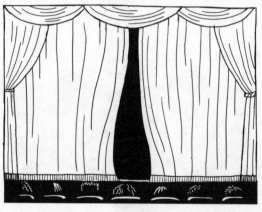

How did you make music from glasses, Susie K?

The glass vibrations cause the air to vibrate, and that creates soundwaves. Different amounts of water create different notes!!

Whatever...

SIGH

We thought the science was cool!!

Thanks, Mr Parkinson. Thanks, Mrs Donald.

And thanks for your help too.

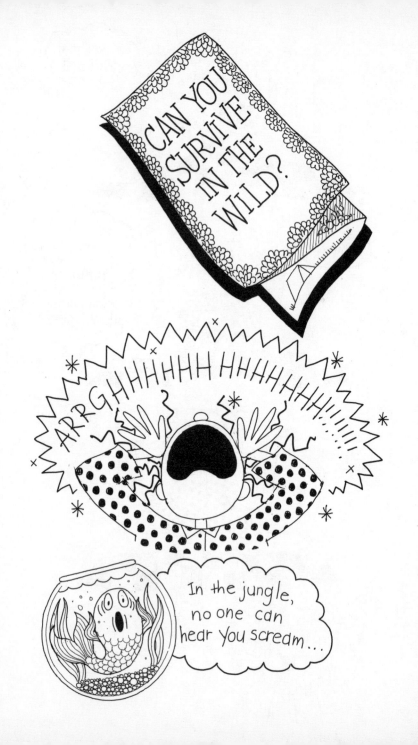

Life of the Party!

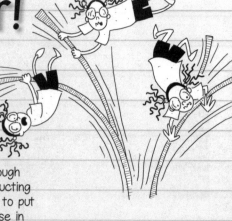

Mum's **REALLY** excited that I'm going to Clementine's party. The only problem is, I haven't been invited **(YET!)** because I'm not exactly the 'life of the party'...

It's a **PROBLEM!** And fortunately **I LOVE** problem-solving. So even though I'd rather stay home and read about endangered animals, I'm going to put my problem-solving skills to use in **OPERATION: LIFE OF THE PARTY!**

Game Changer!

Mum's **OVER THE MOON** that I'm competing in Sports Day at school. The **MAJOR** issue is that I'm hopeless at sports...**ALL** of them!

It's a **PROBLEM!** And fortunately **I LOVE** problem-solving. So even though I'd rather spend the day conducting science experiments, I'm going to put my problem-solving skills to use in **OPERATION: GAME CHANGER!**

The Susie K Diaries

Happy Camper!

Shamini Flint
illustrated by Sally Heinrich

SHAMINI FLINT lives in Singapore with her husband
and two children. She began her career in law in
Malaysia and also worked at an international law firm
in Singapore. She travelled extensively around Asia for
her work, before resigning to be a stay-at-home mum,
writer, part-time lecturer and environmental activist,
all in an effort to make up for her 'evil' past as a
corporate lawyer! Shamini has written many books
for adults and children, including the popular
Diary of a Soccer Star series.

SALLY HEINRICH is an illustrator, printmaker and writer,
who has published and exhibited widely in Australia
and Asia. She has illustrated more than forty books,
including the *Diary of a Soccer Star* series. Her picture
book *One Step at a Time* was an Honour Book in the
CBCA Picture Book of the Year Awards, and her most
recent, *Papa Sky*, is a Notable Book. Her commissioned
artwork ranges from wine labels to a mural for the
Singapore Zoo and community arts projects. Sally has
lived in Singapore, Sydney and Darwin and is now living
in Adelaide. People who have heard her sing are very
happy that she sticks to drawing.